RICKY RICOTTA'S
MIGHTY ROBOT

STORY BY
DAV PILKEY

ART BY
DAN SANTAT

SCHOLASTIC INC.

FOR MIGHTY MEENA AND HER BEST BUDDY, NITRO NIKHIL
– D.P.

FOR ALEK AND KYLE – TWO BROTHERS, AND BEST OF FRIENDS
– D.S.

Library of Congress Cataloging-in-Publication Data

Pilkey, Dav, 1966 – author.
Ricky Ricotta's mighty robot / story by Dav Pilkey ; art by Dan Santat. — Revised edition.
   pages cm
Summary: Ricky Ricotta, a small mouse, is being bullied at school, but when he rescues a powerful robot from its evil creator, he acquires a friend and protector — and saves the city from Dr. Stinky.
1. Mice — Juvenile fiction. 2. Robots — Juvenile fiction. 3. Bullying — Juvenile fiction. 4. Heroes — Juvenile fiction. [1. Mice — Fiction. 2. Robots — Fiction 3. Bullying — Fiction. 4. Heroes — Fiction.] I. Santat, Dan, illustrator. II. Title.
   PZ7.P63123Ro 2014   813.54 — dc23   2013050798

ISBN 978-0-545-63106-8

10 9 8 7 6 5 4 3 2   14 15 16 17 18 19

Printed in China   38

Revised edition
First printing, May 2014

Book design by Phil Falco

CHAPTERS

CHAPTER ONE
RICKY

There once was a mouse named
Ricky Ricotta who lived in
Squeakyville with his mother
and father.

Ricky liked living with
his mother and father, but
sometimes he got lonely.

Ricky wished he had a friend
to keep him company.

"Don't worry," said Ricky's father.
"Someday something **BIG** will happen,
and you will find a friend."
So Ricky waited.

CHAPTER TWO
THE BULLIES

Ricky liked school, but he did not like walking to school. This was because Ricky was very small, and sometimes bullies picked on him.

"Where do you think you are going?" asked one of the bullies.

Ricky did not answer. He turned and started to run.

The bullies chased him.

They knocked Ricky down and threw his backpack into a garbage can.

Every day, the bullies chased Ricky.
Every day, they knocked him down.
And every day, Ricky wished that
something **BIG** would happen.

CHAPTER THREE
DR. STINKY McNASTY

That day at school, Ricky ate lunch by
himself. Then he went outside for recess.

He watched the other mice play a game of kickball. Ricky did not know that something **BIG** was about to happen, but it *was!*

In a secret cave above the
city, a mad doctor was planning
something evil.

Dr. Stinky McNasty had created a Mighty Robot.

"I will use this Robot to destroy the city," said Dr. Stinky, "and soon, I will rule the world!"

Dr. Stinky led his Mighty Robot into town.

"Robot," said Dr. Stinky, "let's have some fun!"

CHAPTER FOUR
THE MIGHTY ROBOT

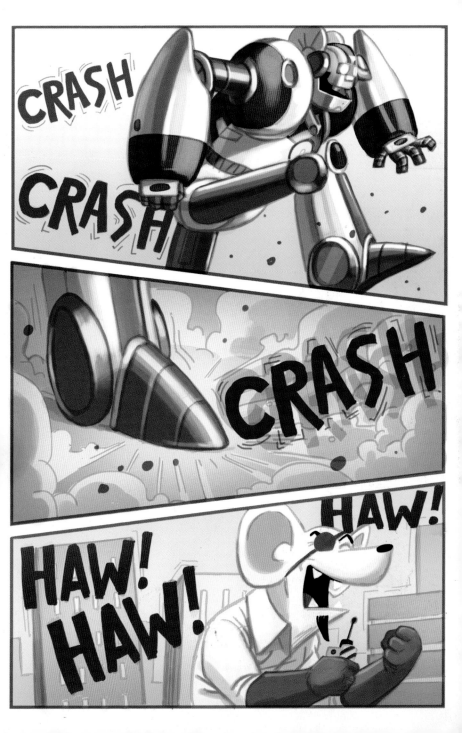

THE MIGHTY ROBOT LOOKED AROUND.

HE SAW THE INNOCENT MICE...

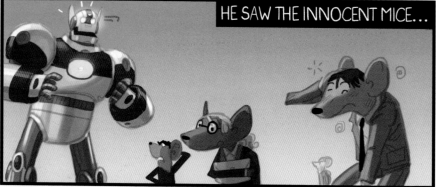

...HE SAW THE FRIGHTENED CHILDREN...

CHAPTER FIVE
RICKY TO THE RESCUE

Dr. Stinky was very angry.

"Destroy Squeakyville!" he cried.
"Destroy Squeakyville!" But the
Robot refused.

"I will teach you a lesson," said Dr. Stinky. He pressed a button on his remote control and zapped the Robot with a terrible shock.

Ricky was watching.

"Stop it!" Ricky cried. But Dr. Stinky kept on zapping the Robot. Finally, Ricky aimed a kickball at the evil doctor. Ricky kicked as hard as he could.

BOING! The kickball bounced off Dr. Stinky's head. Dr. Stinky dropped the controller, and it broke on the ground.

"Rats! Rats! *RATS!*" cried Dr. Stinky. "I shall return!" And he disappeared down a sewer drain.

When the Robot saw what Ricky
had done, he walked over to Ricky.
Everyone screamed and ran.

But Ricky was not afraid. The
Robot smiled and patted Ricky
on the head.

Something **BIG** had happened
after all!

CHAPTER SIX
THE HEROES ARRIVE

That afternoon, the Robot followed
Ricky home from school.

Soon they got to Ricky's house.
"Wait here, Robot," said Ricky.
Ricky went inside.

"Mom, Dad," said Ricky, "can I have a pet?"

"Well," said Ricky's father, "you've been a good mouse lately."

"Yes," said Ricky's mother, "I think a pet would be good for you."

"Hooray!" said Ricky.
"Uh-oh," said Ricky's parents.

CHAPTER SEVEN
RICKY'S MIGHTY ROBOT HELPS OUT

When Ricky's parents saw Ricky's new pet, they were not happy.

"That Robot is too big to be a pet," said Ricky's father.

"There is no room for him in our home," said Ricky's mom.

"But he is my friend," said Ricky, "and he will help us around the house!"

Ricky's Mighty Robot used his super breath to blow all the leaves out of their yard. Ricky's dad liked that.

Ricky's Robot scared all the crows out of the vegetable garden. Ricky's mom liked that.

And when burglars drove by
the Ricottas' house, they kept right
on driving. Everybody liked that!

"Well," said Ricky's father, "I guess your Robot can live in the garage."

"Hooray!" said Ricky.

The next day, Ricky and his Robot walked to school. The bullies were waiting for Ricky.

"Where do you think you're going?" asked one of the bullies.

"My Robot and I are going to school," said Ricky.

The bullies looked up and saw Ricky's Mighty Robot. They were very frightened.

"Um . . . um . . . um . . ." said one
of the bullies. "May we carry your
backpack for you, sir?"

"Sure," said Ricky.

The bullies helped Ricky get to
school safely.

"Is there anything else we can
do for you, sir?" asked the bullies.

"No, thank you," said Ricky.

CHAPTER NINE
SHOW-AND-TELL

That day at school, Ricky's class had show-and-tell. One mouse brought a baseball glove. Another mouse brought a teddy bear.

Ricky brought his Mighty Robot.

Ricky's class got a free ride
on the Robot's back.

They flew up above the
city and over the mountains.

"This is fun!" said Ricky.

CHAPTER TEN
DR. STINKY'S REVENGE

While Ricky's class was flying around in the sky, Dr. Stinky sneaked over to the school. He wanted revenge!

Dr. Stinky crept into Ricky's classroom.
He saw their pet lizard.

"This is just what I need!" said Dr.
Stinky.

He took out a bottle of Hate
Potion #9 and put a drop into
the lizard's water dish. The lizard
drank the water.

Suddenly, the lizard began to
grow and change. He got bigger and
bigger. He got meaner and meaner.

Soon, the lizard turned into an evil monster.

"Destroy Ricky and his Robot!" said Dr. Stinky.

"Yes, Master!" said the monster.

When Ricky's Robot saw the evil monster, he flew down to the school yard. Ricky and his class climbed off quickly. Then, the Robot turned toward the giant creature, and the battle began.

CHAPTER ELEVEN
THE BIG BATTLE

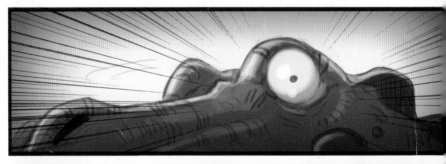

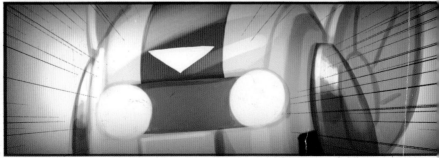

CHAPTER TWELVE
THE FINAL BATTLE
(IN FLIP-O-RAMA™)

FLIP-O
HEY, KIDS! YOU CAN ANIMATE THE ACTION BY FOLLOWING THESE EASY STEPS!

-RAMA
HERE'S HOW IT WORKS!

STEP 1
Place your *left* hand inside the dotted lines marked "LEFT HAND HERE." Hold the book open *flat*.

STEP 2
Grasp the *right-hand* page with your right thumb and index finger (inside the dotted lines marked "RIGHT THUMB HERE").

STEP 3
Now *quickly* flip the right-hand page back and forth until the picture appears to be *animated*.

(For extra fun, try adding your own sound-effects!)

FLIP-O-RAMA 1

(pages 77 and 79)

Remember, flip *only* page 77.
While you are flipping, be sure you
can see the picture on page 77
and the one on page 79.
If you flip quickly, the two
pictures will start to look like
<u>one</u> *animated* picture.

Don't forget to add
your own sound-effects!

LEFT HAND HERE

THE MONSTER ATTACKED.

RIGHT
THUMB
HERE

RIGHT
INDEX
FINGER
HERE

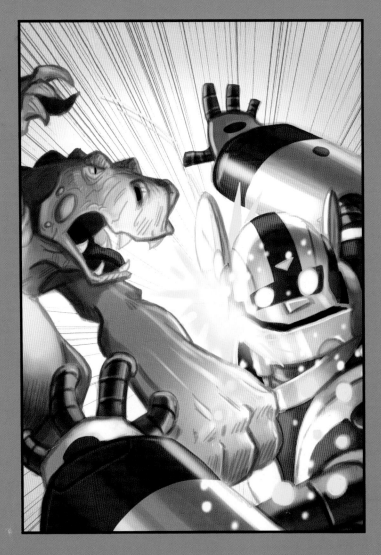

THE MONSTER ATTACKED.

FLIP-O-RAMA 2

(pages 81 and 83)

Remember, flip *only* page 81.
While you are flipping, be sure you
can see the picture on page 81
and the one on page 83.
If you flip quickly, the two
pictures will start to look like
<u>one</u> *animated* picture.

Don't forget to add
your own sound-effects!

LEFT HAND HERE

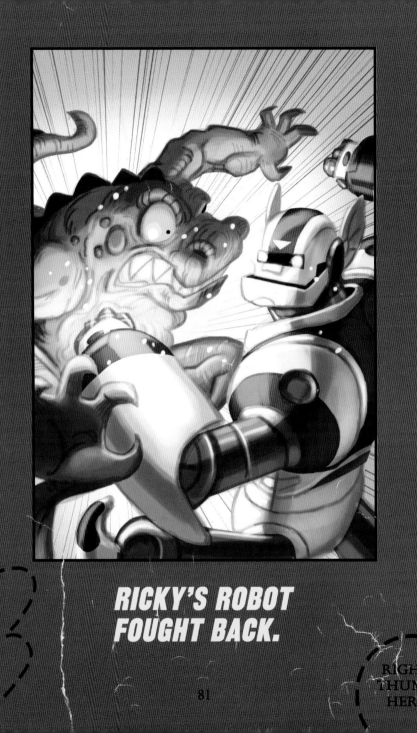

RICKY'S ROBOT
FOUGHT BACK.

RIGHT
THUMB
HERE

RIGHT
INDEX
FINGER
HERE

82

**RICKY'S ROBOT
FOUGHT BACK.**

FLIP-O-RAMA 3

(pages 85 and 87)

Remember, flip *only* page 85.
While you are flipping, be sure you
can see the picture on page 85
and the one on page 87.
If you flip quickly, the two
pictures will start to look like
<u>one</u> *animated* picture.

Don't forget to add
your own sound-effects!

LEFT HAND HERE

THE MONSTER
BATTLED HARD.

RIGHT
THUMB
HERE

86

THE MONSTER
BATTLED HARD.

FLIP-O-RAMA 4

(pages 89 and 91)

Remember, flip *only* page 89.
While you are flipping, be sure you
can see the picture on page 89
and the one on page 91.
If you flip quickly, the two
pictures will start to look like
<u>one</u> *animated* picture.

Don't forget to add
your own sound-effects!

LEFT HAND HERE

**RICKY'S ROBOT
BATTLED HARDER.**

RIGHT
INDEX
FINGER
HERE

90

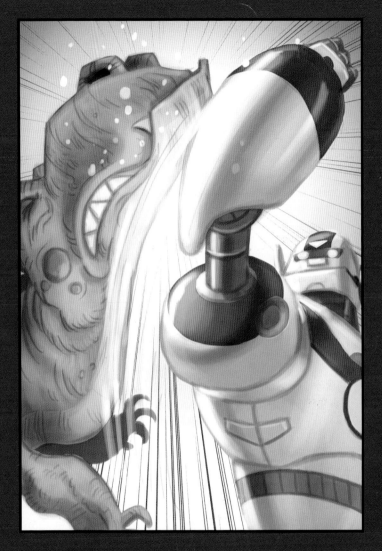

RICKY'S ROBOT
BATTLED HARDER.

FLIP-O-RAMA 5

(pages 93 and 95)

Remember, flip *only* page 93.
While you are flipping, be sure you
can see the picture on page 93
and the one on page 95.
If you flip quickly, the two
pictures will start to look like
<u>one</u> *animated* picture.

Don't forget to add
your own sound-effects!

LEFT HAND HERE

**RICKY'S ROBOT
SAVED THE DAY.**

RIGHT
THUMB
HERE

94

**RICKY'S ROBOT
SAVED THE DAY.**

CHAPTER THIRTEEN
THE ELECTRO-ROCKET

The monster was defeated, and all
of his evil powers went away. Soon,
he turned back into a tiny lizard
and never bothered anybody again.

"Rats! Rats! *RATS!*" cried Dr. Stinky. "I will destroy that Robot myself!" He took his Electro-Rocket and aimed it at Ricky's Robot.

"NO!" screamed Ricky. He leaped onto Dr. Stinky just as the evil doctor fired his rocket.

Up, up, up went the rocket.
Ricky's Robot flew after it. But
he was not fast enough.

The rocket came down and exploded.
Ka-BOOM!
Right on Dr. Stinky's secret cave.

CHAPTER FOURTEEN
JUSTICE PREVAILS

"Rats! Rats! *RATS!*" cried Dr. Stinky. "This has been a bad day for me!"

"It is about to get worse," said Ricky.

Ricky's Mighty Robot picked up Dr.
Stinky and put him in the city jail.

CHAPTER FIFTEEN
BACK HOME

That night, the Ricotta family had a
cookout in the backyard. Ricky told
his mom and dad all about their
adventures that day.

"Thank you for saving the city," said Ricky's father.

"And thank you for saving each other," said Ricky's mother.

"No problem," said Ricky . . .

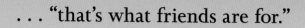

. . . "that's what friends are for."

READY FOR

MORE RICKY?

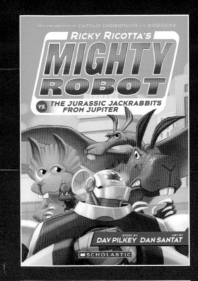

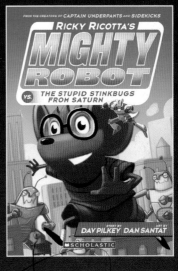

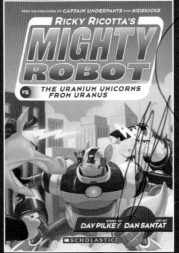

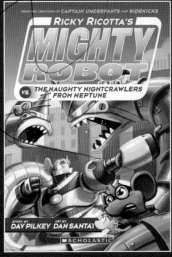

DAV PILKEY

has written and illustrated more than fifty books for children, including *The Paperboy*, a Caldecott Honor book; *Dog Breath: The Horrible Trouble with Hally Tosis*, winner of the California Young Reader Medal; and the IRA Children's Choice Dumb Bunnies series. He is also the creator of the *New York Times* best-selling Captain Underpants books. Dav lives in the Pacific Northwest with his wife. Find him online at www.pilkey.com.

DAN SANTAT

is the writer and illustrator of the picture book *The Adventures of Beekle: The Unimaginary Friend.* He is also the creator of the graphic novel *Sidekicks* and has illustrated many acclaimed picture books, including the *New York Times* bestseller *Because I'm Your Dad* by Ahmet Zappa and *Crankenstein* by Samantha Berger. Dan also created the Disney animated hit *The Replacements.* He lives in Southern California with his family. Find him online at www.dantat.com.